For Karen Li, who always inspires! —D.K.

To Charlotte, my whirling daughter — J.B.

Whirl

Written by
Deborah Kerbel

Illustrated by
Josée Bisaillon

Owlkids Books

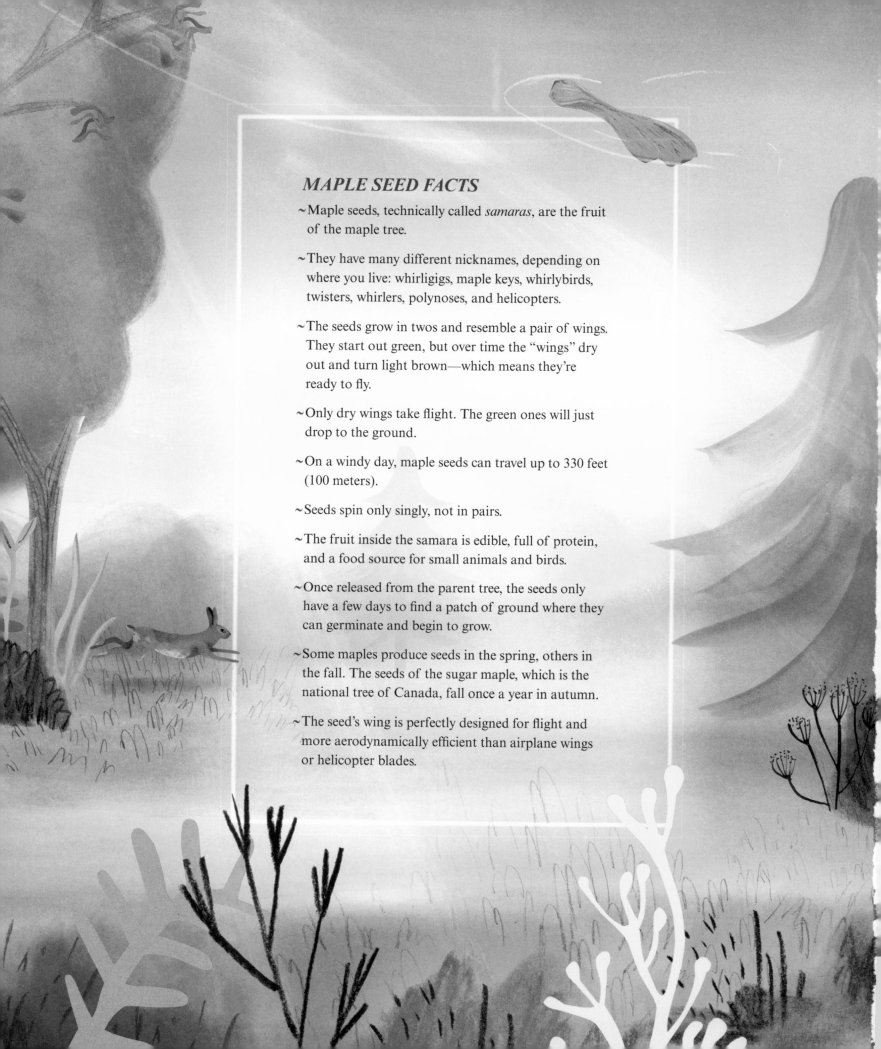

MAPLE SEED FACTS

~ Maple seeds, technically called *samaras*, are the fruit of the maple tree.

~ They have many different nicknames, depending on where you live: whirligigs, maple keys, whirlybirds, twisters, whirlers, polynoses, and helicopters.

~ The seeds grow in twos and resemble a pair of wings. They start out green, but over time the "wings" dry out and turn light brown—which means they're ready to fly.

~ Only dry wings take flight. The green ones will just drop to the ground.

~ On a windy day, maple seeds can travel up to 330 feet (100 meters).

~ Seeds spin only singly, not in pairs.

~ The fruit inside the samara is edible, full of protein, and a food source for small animals and birds.

~ Once released from the parent tree, the seeds only have a few days to find a patch of ground where they can germinate and begin to grow.

~ Some maples produce seeds in the spring, others in the fall. The seeds of the sugar maple, which is the national tree of Canada, fall once a year in autumn.

~ The seed's wing is perfectly designed for flight and more aerodynamically efficient than airplane wings or helicopter blades.

Owlkids Books acknowledges the financial support of the Canada
Council for the Arts, the Ontario Arts Council, the Government of
Canada through the Canada Book Fund (CBF) and the Government
of Ontario through the Ontario Creates Book Initiative for our
publishing activities.

Published in Canada by Owlkids Books Inc.
1 Eglinton Avenue East, Toronto, ON M4P 3A1

Published in the US by Owlkids Books Inc.
1700 Fourth Street, Berkeley, CA 94710

Library of Congress Control Number: 2021939092

Library and Archives Canada Cataloguing in Publication

Title: Whirl / written by Deborah Kerbel ; illustrated by Josée Bisaillon.
Names: Kerbel, Deborah, author. | Bisaillon, Josée, illustrator.
Identifiers: Canadiana 2021022231X | ISBN 9781771474283 (hardcover)
Classification: LCC PS8621.E75 W55 2021 | DDC jC813/.6—dc23

The artwork in this book was created with a mix of collage, drawing
and digital montage.

Edited by Karen Li and Debbie Rogosin
Designed by Alisa Baldwin

Manufactured in Shenzhen, Guangdong, China, in October 2021,
by C&C Offset   Job #HV4342

A   B   C   D   E   F

  Publisher of Chirp, Chickadee and OWL
www.owlkidsbooks.com

Owlkids Books is a division of